AF417062

J.C. HULSEY BOOKS

THE OLD MAN
A Western Short Story

J.C. HULSEY

For information contact: jchulsey1@att.net

Cover Art by Edward Martin
Cover Design by D. Nicolas at www.auroradesigner.com
April 2015
10 9 8 7 6 5 4 3 2 1

ACKNOWLEDGMENTS

A very special Thank You to Ed Martin.
A brand-new friend. Thanks Ed

CHAPTER ONE

Rickety Springs, Wire Rim County, Texas - 1878

Brian Cavanaugh shook his head as he contemplated what the date was. It was his birthday. Brian has just reached the half century mark in his life. People have always said if a professional gunfighter lives past fifty, he is either very good or very lucky. At this age, Brian has decided to hang up his gun and retire. So, he started traveling across the country to return to the place where he had the happiest days in his life and live out the rest of his life in a peaceful environment.

However, life isn't always fair, or maybe it is. Perhaps a person has to atone for his past sins before he can live in peace. Brian stands six feet four inches, has graying hair that at one time was brown in color. His gunmetal gray eyes are the color of his six shooter and can cut a person down, almost as fast as his pistol, with his glare. His body is thicker than it was as a young man, but his reflexes are just as fast, if not faster. It took years of practice to hone his skills. He has a keen eye and can bring down an opponent at sixty yards without any problem.

It was rumored that Wild Bill Hickok shot a man in the heart, seventy-five yards away, with on old ball and cap. 36 caliber pistol. However, that isn't called a rumor for no reason. Legends have always been able to shoot better than normal folks.

Cavanaugh killed his first man when he was twenty-two years old.

~~~~~~~~~~~~~~

I had been enjoying a drink at the local watering hole and accidentally brushed against a man's arm causing him to spill his drink. Words were exchanged and a challenge was thrown out. Being young and uneducated in the ways of the world, I accepted the challenge and stepped out into the street.

I had only been wearing my Colt .45 Peacemaker a little over a month, but every chance I got I would go into the woods and practice, not only shooting straight, but also perfecting my fast draw. I was sure I was as fast as anybody else.

I stepped into the street first and put the sun at my back.

It was a hot Texas sun about halfway down in the sky. I could see that the glare was blinding the other man. I took my gunman's stance that I had been practicing for weeks. I could feel the fear of the situation I had gotten myself into. Sweat started running down between my shoulder blades.

"Oh, Lord, I don't want to die. Please, if you'll just get me out of this, I promise I'll live a good life."

The other man reached for his gun and my slug tore into his body, entering just to the right of the center of his chest. His hand released the gun that he had barely gotten
~~~~~~~~~~~~~~

out of his holster. He looked down at the hole that was leaking blood into his shirt, then looked at me with a scared look on his face. He crumpled to the ground in a heap. His body jerked a few times and then lay still.

CHAPTER TWO

I returned my pistol to my holster just as the sheriff ran up.

"Alright, Cavanaugh. Let's go."

"Go where. It was self-defense. Ask anybody. They all saw it."

"Let's talk about it in my office. Come on."

"You know what? I don't think I will. I didn't do nothing wrong and I ain't going to jail."

"I'm asking you nice to come along. Just because you outshot that pilgrim don't make you a fast gun. Come along. I won't ask again."

"And if I don't?" I started backing away. When I was probably ten feet away, I assumed my gunfighter stance that had served me so well only minutes ago.

"You don't wanna do this?" he warned. "I'm faster than you. There's no reason for you to die."

"Who says I'm gonna die?" I said. "Make your play."

It was like everything slowed to a crawl. I saw the tick in his eye just before his hand started for his revolver. My gun was in my hand, cocked and fired before his gun cleared leather. He finished the draw, but didn't have the strength to raise his gun to fire. He slumped forward and fell to his knees, then fell onto his face in the dusty street.

"Did you see that?" someone said. "The Cavanaugh kid outdrew the sheriff. Faster than a lightning strike. I never seen nothing like it. Man, he's the fastest I ever seen. I shore ain't gonna make him mad at me."

I slid my gun back into the holster, turned and looked around at the gawking crowd, puffed out my chest feeling I was ten feet tall. I started walking away from the two dead bodies lying in the street. I could hear the whispers from the crowd as they parted to let me pass.

That was my first time to take another human being's life, but it wasn't the last. I was a big man in town after that episode. I couldn't even buy my own drinks. I was a big man, a celebrity. I was as famous as Wild Bill Hickok.

A few days later I was leaning my chair back against the wall of the post office with my feet propped up on the rail in front. If somebody came down the sidewalk, they would detour around me so as not to disturb me.

I felt like a king. All I needed was a throne. As I sat there with the brim of my hat shading my eyes against the afternoon sun, I noticed a shadow from under my hat pass over me and blocked out that sun. I pushed my hat back and raised my eyes to see what was disturbing the sunlight. I saw a big black stallion standing in front of the hitch rail.

I raised my eyes a little more and there was a big man dressed all in black, sitting on that black horse. I, also, noticed his silver inlaid holster with a pearl handled gun sticking out.

"You Kid Cavanaugh?" he asked.

"Who wants to know?" I slammed the chair legs down onto the wooden boardwalk, and stood up.

"You killed my brother and now I'm gonna kill you."

"Listen, Stranger," I said calmly. "I don't know you or your brother."

"Sheriff Brent Vermillion was my brother," he countered. "They tell me you shot and killed him. You musta shot him in the back. Couldn't nobody alive take Brent in a fair fight? He was faster than me."

"It was a fair fight," I told him. "You can ask anybody. They'll tell you."

"I don't need to ask anybody. I knew my brother and I know how fast he was. Now, reach."

I was fast. Faster than this so-called fast gun that rode into my town. Just like the two before him, his gun barely cleared leather before the bullet from my gun knocked him back off his horse. The big black jumped and kicked at the body that had fallen back under its legs. The horse started stomping the dead man as the smell of fresh blood covered the ground. The crowd started milling around after they saw the gunman hit the ground.

"Somebody pull that body out from under that horse!" shouted a man.

"You know who he was?" asked another.

"I heard him say he was the brother of the sheriff," said the first man.

"Yeah," said the second man. "But he was also the famous Vermillion Kid. They say he's killed mor'en ten men. Said he was the one taught his brother how to shoot."

"Didn't do either one of them any good, did it?" commented the first man. Somebody call the undertaker."

"The Kid must have a deal with him. Reckon he's gittin' a kickback?" asked the second man.

"Hush," said the first man. "0He'll hear you."

I turned the cylinder, pushed the spent cartridge out and replaced it with a new one.

'Did I really just kill a professional gunman? Am I really that fast?

I know. You're probably wondering about my promise to the Lord right before I had my first gunfight. You know how you always promise something when you get in trouble, but I reckon the Lord knows you ain't gonna keep it. I'll do better when I'm a little older. '

The town council and the mayor came to see me the day after I shot Vermillion.

"Listen Mr. Cavanaugh," said the mayor. "We held a meeting and we have a request for you."

"Yeah," I sneered. "What can I do for you?"

"We want you to leave town," explained the mayor. "With you here, every low life trying to make a reputation for himself is going to show up and there'll be gunplay. It won't be safe to be on the streets."

"What if I don't want to leave?" I asked him.

"We've considered that possibility," he said. "So we made up a little going away present for you. Inside this envelope is five thousand dollars. Enough to set you up in another location. We hope and pray that you will accept our generous offer and find another place to live."

"Five thousand dollars is a lot of money," I said. "Why don't I just take the money and stay right here?"

"I'm afraid it wouldn't be safe for you in this town any longer," he said. "Not only would you have to worry about drifters coming to town, but the townsfolk have decided if you don't leave, then the council cannot be held responsible for your welfare. We firmly suggest that it's in your best interest to take the money and run, so to speak."

I reached and took the envelope, opened the flap and looked inside.

"Whew!" I said. "I didn't know there was this much money in the whole wide world. I'll gather my things and be gone by sundown. Would that be satisfactory, gentlemen?"

"That'll be fine," said the mayor. "Thank you for cooperating."

I went to the boarding house, gathered my things and stuffed them in a small sack. I walked to the livery stable to get my horse.

Albert Kincaid, the livery stable owner was a jovial gray-haired man in his fifties. His bright green eyes crinkled when he smiled at a person and he always had a smile for everybody.

He had let me hang around the stable ever since I was a kid. When I got old enough, he let me go to work for him. I even stayed in his home with him and his wife on many occasions. They were never blessed with children so they treated me like I was their child.

I suppose you're wondering about my own home. It wasn't a happy place. My pa was a big brute of a man who abused my ma and me. Actually, he was my step daddy. My real pa had been killed in a hunting accident when I was five. Ma married Luther Cavanaugh six months later. I took his name as mine, 'cause it made it easier, than having to explain why my last name was different than my pa.

"Howdy, Brian," said Kinkaid. "I reckon it's okay for me to call you Brian 'cause I knowed you since you was a wee little lad. I heard a rumor you was leaving town?"

"Ain't no rumor," I told him. "Wanna git Ranger for me?"

"Sure will. He's a real fine animal. You wouldn't wanna swap him, would you? He asked. "I got a real nice mare in the corral out back. You orta take a look. I'll give fifty and the mare for Ranger."

"Albert, you try to trade with me every time I come in here," I told him. "The answer is always the same and it ain't no different this time. Just get my horse please?"

"Okay. It don't hurt none to ask again. You got any idea where you might be heading?" he asked.

"I thought I might head west, or maybe east. They say East Texas has a lot of green trees and lakes full of bass and catfish," I said. "Hell, I don't know where I'm going. I'll let Ranger take me wherever. How's that sound to you?"

"I, fer one, am gonna miss that ugly mug of yours. You take care, you hear? Why, you're just like kin to me. You was a lot of help around here 'afore you got famous and all. Shucks, I'm gonna start blubbering like a baby. Go on," he said. "Git outa here."

I smoothed the blanket out over Ranger's back, threw the saddle across, reached underneath and tightened the cinch. I turned and offered my hand to Albert. He shook it with his callused one. He nodded at me and turned away. I believe I saw him lift a hand to brush at his eyes.

I put my left foot into the stirrup, pulled myself up, swung my leg over and settled into the saddle. I touched my hat brim, gave Ranger a free rein, nudged him with my knees and we took off.

CHAPTER THREE

We traveled until midnight, then made camp, in a little arroyo, next to a small creek. I tethered Ranger to a little bush in a patch of tall grass after letting him fill up on water. I gathered enough sticks and leaves and started a fire and made a pot of coffee and set it next to the flame. While it was heating, I rolled out my bedroll using my saddle for a pillow. It had been quite a while since I had slept on the cold hard ground, and I wasn't looking forward to it tonight. I poured myself a cup of coffee, leaned against my saddle and crossed my ankles.

What was I doing out here in the middle of nowhere? Where was I going? A man needs a plan. He needs a place to call home. Well, I'll think about that problem tomorrow. I dumped the few drops of coffee that was left in my cup, pulled the blanket up for cover and closed my eyes. The next thing I knew was a feeling in my left side. It felt like somebody was kicking me. I opened my eyes and looked up at the biggest, ugliest man I had ever seen.

From down here on the ground, he looked like a giant. I stood up and he wasn't quite as tall, although he was close to seven feet. He towered over my six feet four inch frame. He was dressed in homemade pants and a feed sack shirt. Size extra-large. His hat was a floppy felt one that had seen its better days.

"You need to wake up Mister," he said. "This here is private property and the boss don't like strangers squatting on his land."

"I ain't squatting," I said. "I just stopped here for the night. I was getting too tired to go any further. I didn't know it was private property. I'll leave just as soon as I have a little something to eat."

"I think you'd better leave now," he said. "The boss don't like strangers on his land."

"Yeah. You told me that," I said. "How about you join me for some bacon and beans? Would you like that?"

"Sure," he said. "I could eat again. You got any coffee?"

"There should be some in the pot there, but it's cold." I told him. "Grab some sticks, get the fire going and heat it up."

When it was hot, he reached down, picked up the coffee pot by the hot handle without flinching and poured a cup full.

"Didn't that burn your hand?" I asked surprised.

"What, burn my hand?" he questioned. "What you talking about?"

"Nothing," I said. "I was talking to myself." *Did he really not feel that hot handle?'* I dumped some beans and bacon in a skillet and stirred them around until they were hot.

"Grab a couple of plates over there," I told him. "Let's eat this while it's hot."

He came back with two tin plates and a couple of spoons. I wrapped my bandana around my hand, picked up the hot skillet and dished about half the beans and bacon into his plate.

"I'll just eat out of the skillet." I sat it down on the rock next to my saddle and started spooning it into my mouth.

"You got some more?" he asked looking at the skillet.

"Here, take mine. I ain't too hungry anyway." I handed the skillet to him. He grabbed the hot handle with his big hand.

"Got any more?" he asked belching loudly.

"Sorry, Pal, that was it," I said. "I wasn't planning on having a guest for breakfast."

"You go now," he said placing the skillet on the ground. "Boss don't like."

"Yeah, yeah, I know," I said. "Let me gather up these things and I'm out of your hair."

"Roscoe don't got hair." With those words he took off his floppy hat and revealed a shiny bald head as big as a watermelon.

"It's just a figure of speech. Oh, what's the use? I'm going. You tell your boss, I appreciate his hospitality."

"What? Appre.. hospit..?"

"Forget it, Roscoe. I'll see you on down the trail."

"You don't come back here. Boss don't like..."

His voice trailed off as I got further away. "What a strange man. At least he didn't hurt me." I rubbed my ribs where he had kicked me.

CHAPTER FOUR

Ranger and I were enjoying the scenery. The smell of the lush green forest of cedar trees. They went as far to the east as I could see. Off to the right was open prairie filled with rye grass, dotted with Blue Bonnets and Red Indian Paintbrush swaying with the breeze coming from the north. It was a cool wind, which I enjoyed this time of year. A lot better than the hot Texas sun beating down on me all the time.

Speaking of the sun.

"Where is it? There you are, behind that little cloud. You can stay there for a little longer as far as I'm concerned."

I looked at the trail ahead of us and saw a couple of horses coming our direction. I pulled up on Ranger's reins and waited. I reached down and removed the leather tie down on the hammer of my gun. Man can't be too careful. They stopped about five feet from me. Their horses were covered with lather. They were traveling fast from someplace.

The one on the lead horse was skinny, had a hawk face with a goat-tee, long greasy hair hanging to his collar. The other fellow was sitting short in the saddle, wearing a bowler. He kept looking from me to his partner. He seemed extremely nervous. The first man spoke, his voice had a Yankee sound to it.

"Howdy, stranger," he said. "Where you headed?"

"Don't you know it's impolite to ask a man that question?" I said.

"Don't mean nothing by it. Just being friendly is all. Did you come from South of here?"

"There you go again with the questions. Too many questions can get a man hurt or even dead, if you know what I mean?"

"Boy, you sure are one touchy dude, ain't you?"

"I'm a firm believer in a fellow minding his own business. Now, if you'll excuse me? I'll be heading on down the road."

"Hold on!" he said with his Yankee voice. "I've got one more question fer you?"

The slug from my pistol knocked him off his horse and onto the dirt trail. Blood was staining the road as he lay there trying to catch his breath. He coughed, blood spraying from his mouth. He groaned once and then was silent.

"Don't shoot," yelled the nervous man. "I didn't even pull my weapon. See. It's still in the holster. Please Mister."

"I ain't gonna shoot you, but you need to take two fingers, lift your gun out of the holster and toss it down next to your buddy."

"Sure. I'm doing exactly as you say. See. I throwed it on the ground."

I changed the spent cartridge with a new one and holstered my pistol.

"Tell me something?" I asked him. "Are you boys running from the law or something?"

"It ain't the law. It's Marylou's daddy. Bufford took advantage of her against her will last night and her daddy said he was gonna hang him from the highest tree he could find. I hit the trail with him 'cause he's my, well, he was my best friend. I sure would be obliged if you'd let me go on down the road."

"You climb down and load your friend on his pony, then you can go. He didn't need to die, you know, but he shouldn't have gone for his gun."

"If it wouldn't make you mad, could you tell me your name? I'd like to know who killed my friend."

"Name's Brian Cavanaugh. Some folks call me Kid Cavanaugh. Maybe you heard of me?"

"Sure," he said. "I heard about you. You killed the Vermillion Kid and his brother that was sheriff. I shore wish Bufford had known that before he threw down on you."

"Adios," he said. "Maybe I'll see you again someday under better circumstances."

"Maybe so," I nodded my head and said, "So long."

He was climbing off his horse as I rode past him and his dead friend.

Is this the way it's gonna be from now on? Is there always gonna be somebody that wants to die? Wonder how far to the next town?

I noticed a cloud of dust on the trail ahead.

CHAPTER FIVE

'Must be Marylou's daddy coming after Bufford. Reckon he'll be disappointed that I saved him the trouble of hanging him?'

I pulled up and waited for the riders.

"Whoa! Did you pass a couple of fellows riding fast?" asked the leader of the group.

"I did," I answered.

"Well, how far ahead are they?" he said quickly. "Speak up, stranger, we're burning daylight."

"One of you gents Marylou's papa?" I asked.

"I'm her father," the leader said. "How you know about Marylou?"

"I sure hope you ain't too disappointed, but Bufford is dead," I told him. "I know you wanted to hang him for what he did to your daughter, but he tried to drop me. He didn't succeed. I'm real sorry."

"How do I know you're telling the truth?" he asked. "You could be friends with them, trying to throw us off their trail."

"Now you've gone and hurt my feelings," I said. "I don't appreciate your accusations. It's downright insulting. I think you owe me an apology."

"You sure talk big for one man," he said. "Take a look around and if you can count, you'll count six riders. The boys ain't just cowhands. They can also handle a gun. Now, I meant no insult, not at all. It's just a man can't be too careful when he's chasing scum like that Bufford Holloway and his friend Glen Johnson. What did you say your name was?"

"There you go again with the questions," I said. "You know that's how Bufford wound up staring up at the sky from flat on his back. Too many questions. However, since you asked so nice, and there are so many of you, I'll tell you my name. It's Brian Cavanaugh outta Rickety Springs. Maybe you heard about me?"

There was a lot of murmuring amongst the riders.

"Are you Kid Cavanaugh?" asked one of the cowboys. "The one shot Kid Vermillion and his sheriff brother?"

"That's me. Pleased to meet you," I said. "What's your name, Marylou's papa?"

"Name's Crawford Pritchett," he said. "I own the CP Ranch, about fifteen miles east of here. I could use a man like you. There's always somebody fussing with me about where my cattle graze or some other problem. You interested in hiring your gun?"

Pritchett was a large man that commanded attention when he spoke. A man who was used to handing out orders, and having them followed to the tee. He was probably in his late forties or early fifties. His hair, what I could see of it under his hat was turning gray. His piercing whisky colored eyes gave no indication as to what he was thinking. He would make a good poker player.

"Never thought about it," I said. "How much does it pay?"

"If you were hiring on to herd my cattle like these boys," he explained. "It would be thirty a month and found, but since you'll have other duties, so to speak, I reckon you would earn seventy-five a month and found. We've got a real good cook, just ask any of the boys."

"I guess I could try it for a while," I said. "I might leave at any time, though. You need to understand that up front."

"That'd be no problem," he said. "Oh! There is one more thing."

"Yeah. What's that?" I asked.

"Marylou is off limits. You're not to approach her or try to talk to her for any reason," He said. "Is that understood?"

"I hear you loud and clear, Boss."

"Let's head back to the ranch," he told them. "Since the Kid here took care of our little problem."

I fell in behind them as they turned their mounts and headed east.

'Well, it's official. I'm a hired gun. I don't feel no different than I did before. What is it about this Marylou that he's so protective? If she's a looker, I might have a hard time following that order to stay away from her. I'd sure hate to cross the boss, but a young man has to have his fun.'

We passed through a gate with a big sign hanging down that read CP RANCH. Cattle bought and sold. We rode for what seemed like a mile or so when I saw a big sprawling house. I had never seen a house as big as this one. It was a two-story brick house with a covered porch across the front. There were flower beds and trees, decorating the yard in front and on both sides. It was very impressive.

"You boys go about your business. You've got a lot of things to catch up on," Pritchett told the men. "Kid, you come inside with me. Vic, put my horse up and take care of the Kid's horse too."

"Yes, sir, Boss," said Vic.

Vic led the horses along with his own horse across the yard toward the large red barn. Another impressive structure. Mr. Pritchett must do pretty well at this cattle business.

"Come on inside, Kid. I need to show you a map of the spread. It'll show you the spots where we've been having trouble. Tomorrow I'll ride out with you and explain a little more about what I want you to do."

We walked through the front door and a Mexican woman took Pritchett's hat.

"Your hat, Senor?" she held out her small hand. I removed my hat and placed it in her hand. She nodded and backed away.

"In here Kid. This is where I conduct all my business. You want a whisky?"

"Yes, please if you don't mind. I'd like a whisky."

He poured about three fingers into two glasses and handed one to me. The walls of the room were covered with bookshelves filled with books. I didn't know there were this many books in the entire world.

"You read all these books, Boss?"

"I've read the majority of them. Do you read, Kid?"

"Naw. Never had much of an opportunity. Sure would like to though."

"You're welcome to pick out your choice of a book any time you're not conducting Ranch business. A young man should always broaden his education. Books are one of the greatest ways to do that."

"Thank you, sir. I believe I'll take you up on that offer."

"Now come over here to the desk and let's take a look at those maps. We've got almost two thousand acres. Most of its open range, but we have deeded land also.

There are neighbors on three sides that think they have as much right to the land as I do."

"I understood that's what open range is. Open range."

"You're right. It is open, but the unwritten law is that the first one to claim it has the right to claim it as his range. I've had cattle on it for almost ten years and now my neighbors have decided to move me off and put their stock on it. That ain't gonna happen. Not as long as I have a breath in my body. Now, you'll eat with us, won't you?"

"You don't want me to eat in the bunkhouse with the rest of the hands?"

"There'll be time enough for that tomorrow. I want you to meet my daughter. You already know her name."

'Now why would he want me to meet his daughter, when he told me to stay away from her?'

We walked across the hall into a spacious dining room. The table was long, with enough chairs to seat a dozen people easily. In the middle of the table sat a hunk of meat that looked like half a cow. I know I'm exaggerating, but it was big and the aroma was heavenly. It made my mouth water and my stomach growl.

"Sounds like you're hungry. Please be seated and we'll eat soon as Marylou gets here. Ah. Here she is."

I stood as she entered the room. I had never seen a more beautiful girl. Pale white skin with pale blue eyes, blonde hair pulled up on top of her head. A cotton dress covered with blue flowered decorations swaying with her perfect five-foot figure as she walked to the table. Indeed I was going to have a hard time staying away from this lovely creature.

"Marylou, this is Kid. What's your first name again?"

"Brian, ma'am. Brian Cavanaugh. Pleased to make your acquaintance." I was having a hard time getting the words out of my mouth.

"Brian is going to be working for me. I wanted you to meet him. I will probably have him accompany you when you go to town."

"Oh Papa, I don't need anyone to babysit me. I can take care of myself." Her velvety voice almost made me want to melt.

"Have you forgotten what just happened to you?" he asked her.

"No, Papa. I haven't forgotten. I suppose you're right as always," she conceded.

Pritchett picked up a little bell and rang it. A different Mexican woman entered the room.

"Yes sir?" she asked.

"You may serve us now, Adriana," said Pritchett

"Right away, sir," she started carrying dishes around the table and asked each one of us if we wanted this item. It was something I had never seen before. The meal was tastier than anything I had eaten in any café or restaurant anyplace.

"This meal is very good, sir," I said. "May I have another piece of that scrumptious roast beef?"

"Adriana. Serve more meat to our guest," he told the woman."

"Yes, sir," she carried the platter around the table and held it to my side. "More meat, sir?"

"Thank you, Adriana," I told the woman. "It's very good."

"You don't need to thank her. She's not the one who cooked the meal," said Pritchett. "She's just a maid."

"She can tell the cook how much I enjoyed it, can't she?" I asked him.

"Of course," he said. "Adriana, tell Chiquita our guest enjoyed the meal," he then turned back to me. "Would you like to retire to the drawing room for another glass of whisky?"

"If it's all the same to you, sir, I think I'd like to retire for the night," I told him. "Where am I to sleep? In the bunkhouse?"

"No, I don't think so," he said. "I believe I'd like to keep you closer. You can take a bedroom upstairs. The second door on the right. Goodnight Kid."

"Goodnight Sir. Goodnight Miss Pritchett."

"Please call me Marylou," she said.

"Only if you call me Brian," I told her.

"Goodnight, Brian," she purred.

"Goodnight Marylou." I could swear I saw her wink with one of those blue eyes.

I climbed the stairs and went into the second room on the right. It was almost as big as the whole house that the Kincaids lived in. The bed had a canopy around it. I was almost afraid to lay down in it.

'It's only a bed and that's what beds are made for. To sleep in.' I splashed water on my face, removed my clothes and climbed into that feather soft mattress. I was asleep in a matter of seconds.

I was awakened by the sound of someone knocking on the door. I got out of bed and opened the door. When I saw Marylou, I closed the door, so she couldn't see me in my drawers.

"Let me in," she begged.

"I can't let you in," I said. "I'm not dressed."

"I don't mind if you don't. Please let me in," she continued to beg. "I want to talk to you."

"Can't it wait till morning?" I asked.

"Come on, Brian, you're not afraid of a girl, are you?"

"I'm not afraid of you. I'm afraid of myself. You're the most beautiful girl I've ever seen."

"Let me in and I'll show you more of that beauty."

"Ok. But don't say I didn't warn you."

I opened the door and she rushed by me. I stuck my head out and looked up and down the hallway. It wouldn't do for Pritchett to find her in my room in the middle of the night.

"You look even better in your under drawers. Come closer so we can get better acquainted."

"You do realize what your daddy would do if he found you in my room?"

"I imagine you would act differently than Bufford. He just tucked his tail and ran like a scared rabbit. I don't think you would do that. Would you?" She fluttered those long lashes at me and I felt my knees start to buckle.

She walked toward me. I backed against the edge of the bed. She reached with her little hand and pushed. I landed on my back. She flung herself on top of me. What's a man supposed to do in a situation like this?

I allowed her to press her smooth, tasty red lips against mine. She reached and slipped her hand under the top of my drawers. I was lost. She could do anything she wanted to with me.

~~~~~~~~~~~~~~
~~~~~~~~~~~~~~

I heard her get out of bed and dress a little later. She opened the door and slipped into the hallway, pulling the door closed behind her.

'What have I done? If Pritchett finds out it won't make any difference that it was her idea? Maybe I need to consider moving on. I don't need the money. That girl ain't no girl, she's a grown woman and a very special one at that, but I don't need to let this happen again.'

~~~~~~~~~~~~~~~~

"Good morning Kid," said Pritchett. "Did you rest well?"

"I enjoyed it very much," I told him. "Thank you for asking."

Marylou looked up from the table and her eyes twinkled with our secret. Those eyes of hers could mesmerize a man. I needed to get out of this house.

"Sit down and enjoy some eggs and sausage," Pritchett said.

"I need to go check on my horse. Maybe I'll get a bite after." I turned without looking at Marylou, walked out the door and headed for the big barn.
~~~~~~~~~~~~~~~~

CHAPTER SIX

I located Ranger, saddled him, mounted and rode out the barn door, down the road to the big gate and onto the trail that I should have been traveling without any detours.

'What an experience that was. How many miles is it to a town? I hope not too far. I'm hungry after last night and then not eating this morning.'

About two hours passed and I saw some buildings. It wasn't a large town.

'Surely I can get something to ease this gnawing in my gut.'

I kicked Ranger in the sides and we galloped to the Main Street heading into town. I reined back and stopped. The sign said Rascal Flats Pop 457. That was crossed out and under it was scrawled 456. That was crossed out and 455. It seemed there was an epidemic in town. Folks were either dying or moving away. I guided Ranger down the Main Street and stopped in front of the livery stable. A sign over the door read. Lister's Livery Stable. Horses boarded, bought and sold. I dismounted and led Ranger over to the water trough. He bent down and slurped his fill. I bent down next to him, removed my hat and dunked my head under the cool water.

"Hello, stranger," said the livery man. "You wanna board your horse?"

"I reckon I do," I told him. "How much?"

"Depends," he said. "How long you figure you gonna be in town? It's cheaper the longer you leave him."

"How about a week," I said. "How much for one week?"

"That'd be four dollars. If'n I had charged the daily rate it would'd been a dollar a day. Gets cheaper the longer he stays."

"Yeah. I heard the first time. Where can I get a bite to eat?"

"Only food in town is at the Lonely Dog Saloon. Ain't too tasty, but it's filling."

"Thanks. Don't overfeed him with grain. Just a cup of oats and all the hay he wants."

I walked out of the stable, turned and watched Lister lead Ranger inside. I sure liked that horse. He's the best friend I got right now. I turned back around and walked across the street to the saloon. I stopped just outside the double doors and peered over the top. There were seven round tables with four chairs at each table. Two of the tables were occupied. Four at one, two at another. They were dressed like drovers. Each table had a bottle of rotgut sitting in the center. The cowboys were each nursing a glass. When a glass was empty, the man would reach for the bottle and refill his glass. None of them seemed to be in any hurry.

I pushed through the door, stepped to the side and stopped. Every head turned my direction. I could feel apprehension in their eyes as they only saw the gun tied to my leg. I nodded and stepped to the bar.

"Can I get something to eat?" I asked the bartender.

"Sure," he answered. "We got sandwiches or Venison stew."

"Is the stew, fresh?" I asked.

"'Bout a week old," He said. "It's filling, that's all I can say 'bout it. You want a bowl?"

"Let me have it with a cold beer, I'll be at that table over in the rear." I pointed to a table in the back of the room.

"Ain't got no cold beer. It's lukewarm, but it'll quench your thirst."

"I'll take one to the table with me. If you got it, I'd like some bread with the stew." He drew a beer and slid it to me.

"Bread comes with the stew," he said.

I carried my beer and threaded my way through the other tables.

"Say, don't I know you?" asked one of the cowboys. "Sure. You're Kid Cavanaugh. I thought you went to work for Crawford Pritchett over at the CP Ranch?"

"I decided I wasn't cut out for ranch work," I said.

"Did you meet his daughter, Marylou?" he asked.

"We met," I said.

"She's a corker, ain't she?" he said.

"Man shouldn't talk about a lady like that," I said calmly.

"What'd you mean?" he snorted. "Marylou sure ain't no lady. Maybe she's the reason you moved on. Am I right?"

"You know I never did like too many questions," I told him. "I only came in here for a bite to eat. I don't care much for conversing with morons."

"Them's fighting words," he stood.

"As I said, I came in here to eat, nothing more. However, if you want to push it, I can oblige you."

"You sorry SOB. I'm gonna break you in two." He made a move toward me and the next thing I heard from him as he got off the floor was,

"Why'd you hit me with your gun?" he whined. "Can't you fight like a normal person? You just don't whack a man up side his head with your gun."

"In my line of work, I can't afford to hurt my hands. You're lucky I only tapped you. If you don't like what I did, keep that in mind next time you start shooting off your mouth."

"Never seen a man wouldn't fight with his fists," he continued whining.

"You have now. Now, you got any more smart words?" I looked at him.

"I don't believe I do," he said, "I didn't mean nothing. It's just the whisky talking. I apologize if I offended you."

"I accept your apology," I said. "Now here comes my stew. I'd like to eat it alone."

The drovers stood and left the room, leaving their half full bottles on the tables. One of them rubbing a knot on his head.

The barkeep came from behind the bar and picked up the bottles. He carried them back to the bar and proceeded to pour the remains of one into the other. He then set the full one on the shelf behind the bar.

He shrugged his shoulders at me and said, "Man's gotta save a dollar anyway he can."

I finished the stew and walked to the bar.

"How much I owe you?"

"Two bits. How'd you like it?"

"Like you said, it's filling. Is there a place I can bed down for the night?"

I got a couple rooms upstairs. I used them for my whores, but there wasn't enough business for'em, so they moved on. Dollar a night, and I just changed the sheets last week. Ain't nobody used'em since then."

"Here's two and a quarter. I might stay another night."

"Thanks. My names Luther Crenshaw. I own this fantastic establishment. Did I hear that cowboy call you Kid Cavanaugh?"

"Why you asking?"

"Did you really beat Vermillion to the draw? I seen him onest in Larado. He killed two men before they cleared leather."

"I reckon he slowed down since then. And he's even slower now. Which room?"

"Top of the stairs on your right. Doors not locked, don't even have a lock, in case you need one, prop the chair under the knob."

"See you in the morning. Are we having stew for breakfast or do you have eggs?"

"Eggs, bacon and plenty of black coffee."

I went up the stairs and entered my abode for the night. I had dreams about a beautiful young girl coming into my room. Or was it a dream?

The next morning, I enjoyed a breakfast of bacon, eggs and coffee. It was a lot better than the stew. A whole lot better.

I paid for the breakfast and went outside. It wasn't much of a town. Just a few squatty buildings, nothing fancy and all needing a paint job.

What am I doing here in this one-horse town? I need to head out and find a town where I can maybe buy a cattle ranch or a business. Or maybe I'll try my hand at gambling, although I've never been much good at it. What kind of business would I want to be involved in? I reckon I don't need to worry too much about it right at the moment.

I spent the day strolling around town. That night I tried my hand at poker. Like I said before, I ain't very good at it. I played until sunup, then bade the other player's goodnight and went up to my room.

I was getting ready to lie down, when there was a knock on the door.

CHAPTER SEVEN

"I was hoping you was still here," it was the cowboy I had tapped on the head. "Since you're not working for old Pritchett no more, my boss said he'd like to talk to you about coming to work for him."

"Who's your boss?" I asked.

"Albert Swenson. Maybe you've heard of the Swenson Horse Ranch. It's one of the largest horse ranches in Texas."

"Did Swenson say what he'd be wanting me to do?"

"He didn't tell me, but we've been having trouble with rustling. He probably wants you to take care of that."

"Why can't his hands handle it?"

"We ain't gunmen. We done lost two men 'cause they tried to tangle with them. He feels we need a professional gunman like you."

"I'll ride out with you in the morning. Right now I'm dead tired and all I care about is some rest. I plan on sleeping straight through 'til morning."

"Okay. I'll see you in the morning, meet you at the stable."

"Okay. After breakfast," I said. "Say. How's your head?"

"It's a lot better. The boss got a big laugh outta how you treated me. Said I was lucky you didn't kill me. I'm sure glad you didn't. My head's a lot harder than it looks. See you in the morning."

The next morning, I met the cowboy at the livery stable, picked up Ranger and we rode out to the ranch.

Swenson has a twenty-year-old daughter. Her name is Dakota. She's got beautiful flaming red hair that frames her pearl white face. She's five feet one inch tall, the perfect size for a woman such as her. She dresses in Mexican style dresses with that elastic all around the top. It can be pulled down to show one or both shoulders. It is indeed a very sexy dress. When she smiles it lights up the entire room. She and I became very close and spent many hours together, when I wasn't out on the range. Her father didn't seem to mind, in fact, he seemed to encourage the relationship. Perhaps he was looking for a husband for his daughter.

One day, when I had some time off, I rode to the top of the ridge on the south side of the meadow. It was the most beautiful spot of the whole range.

Dakota and I had spent many hours here. We would sit and talk about what we wanted our life to be in the future. She just assumed that the plans we made was for the two of us as a couple.

We had come mighty close to going all the way on more than one occasion, but I kept finding a reason not to. As much as I cared for her, I couldn't stand the thought of her getting hurt if I got myself shot and killed.

I tied my horse to a tree branch and found a soft spot beneath a big oak tree. I sat down and leaned back against it. I could see the whole valley from here. I hoped one day to have a place as pretty as this. There wasn't any reason I couldn't. I still had the money that the council gave me for leaving town. When I get back to the ranch, I'll tell Swenson that I want to go to town tomorrow. The sooner I found out about this the better. Of course, it would be a lot better if I knew for sure that Dakota would be with me. She would be like icing on the cake. I'm almost certain she would go with me if I asked her.

I scanned the complete horizon again. Yes, a place like this is where I could settle down without the outside world crowding me. But, would I be able to settle down with my reputation as a gunman or would that rob me of the happiness I've been dreaming about?

I glanced up from my daydreaming and saw a man riding a powerful dark Gray stallion through the small stream that ran adjacent to the oak tree, right up to where I was standing. A stranger as far as I knew. Of course, I don't know all that many people in this part of the country. He could easily be a friend of the Swensons. I rested my hand on my pistol.

He sat there with an air of confidence about him. His body fit the saddle as though he was part of it. I looked toward the main house to see if anybody had noticed him. There was no one in sight.

I couldn't tell how tall he was, perched up on his saddle, but I could see he was a big man. His arms were twice the size of mine. Wouldn't want to arm wrestle him.

He pulled up on the reins, lifted his leg over the saddle horn and took out the makings for a smoke. He still hadn't said anything. He spread the tobacco over the thin paper, rolled it with one hand, licked the paper, placed it between his lips, while with the other hand he took out a match. He looked directly at me as he scratched the match on his belt buckle and lifted it to the end of his smoke. He inhaled deeply and tossed the match to the ground. He continued looking at me and puffing his cigarette.

"What'cha doing here, stranger?" I asked. "You know this is Swenson's ranch?"

He still hadn't spoken. He took the last puff off his smoke, pinched the lit end off, then tossed what was left to the ground.

"Nobody told you about me, did they?" he asked with a nasal twang.

"I don't reckon they did. Who are you? I asked that once already."

"My name's Roger Swenson. Nobody never said nothing about a Roger Swenson?"

"Exactly who is Roger Swenson?"

"Why, I am. I'm Cousin Roger from over Adair, County way. I come to visit Uncle Albert and Cousin Dakota. Are you her beau? You're just the type she'd fall for."

"How come you stopped here? Why didn't you ride on to the house?"

"I stopped here when I spotted you relaxing under this big oak tree. This is Dakota's favorite spot of the whole ranch. I bet it's yours too. You coming back to the house with me or you gonna let me surprise them by myself?"

"I reckon I'll walk with you, but if we're gonna walk you need to come down off your horse."

"I'll walk him real slow so's not to get ahead of you. I don't git off my horse till I need to."

"Suit yourself. Let's go." I took off walking ahead of Cousin Roger Swenson. I could hear his horse's hooves as they trampled the grass. We were almost to the main house when Mr. Swenson came running out.

"Roger Swenson. I told you never to set foot on this property again or it'd be too bad for you. What're you doing here?"

"Aw, Uncle Albert, you know you don't mean that? After all, we're kin. Surely you've forgotten all about that little squabble we had over a few head of your precious horses?"

"You stole them horses and sold 'em to pay off your gambling debts. If you'd come to me like a man and asked, I would have given you the money. But, no, you had to help yourself and steal from me. As you said, your own kin. I haven't forgotten. Turn your horse around and move on outa here. You're not welcome here."

"At least, let me say hello to Cousin Dakota?"

"Dakota feels about you the same as me. She don't wanna talk to you."

"Why don't you let her tell me that?"

"Roger, I took you in when your mama, my sister died. That's what you do with kin folks. Treated you like one of my own. Gave you everything. Maybe I was too easy on you. Look how you turned out."

"I ain't all that bad," he whined.

"Roger," I said to him. "I think Mr. Swenson's made himself pretty clear. Maybe you need to do like your Uncle said. Move along."

"Who are you to tell me what to do?" more whining. "This ain't none of your concern."

"I'm making it my business. Now, do you want to discuss it any further?" I rested my hand on my pistol and looked at him with my most intimidating stare.

"Okay. Okay. I'm going, but I do think you should reconsider, Uncle Albert. I could be a real help around here on this ranch."

"Yeah. Help yourself to more horses. No thank you, we don't need you kind of help. Goodbye."

With those words Mr. Swenson turned his back on Cousin Roger and strolled back in the house.

"I always thought blood was thicker than water, so to speak. I guess it ain't true," he said. "So Long. Say I never caught your name?"

"Didn't give it, but, it's Brian Cavanaugh."

"You're Kid Cavanaugh?" he asked surprised.

"You guessed it. Now Kid Cavanaugh suggests you get moving."

"I'm going. Wait till I tell Calvin I met Kid Cavanaugh. He'll never believe me," he turned his mount, kneed him in his sides and left the yard at a gallop. I turned back from watching him disappear toward the house.

Dakota was walking toward me. Her figure was accentuated by the dress she wore. It wasn't the normal one that she usually wore. Her ample bosom filled the upper part of the dress completely. As she walked toward me, my heart seemed to leap into my throat. I tried to swallow, but the lump didn't want to go down. I swallowed a second time before I spoke.

"You're the most beautiful creature I've ever seen."

"I bet you tell all the girls that."

"There's never been one like you. All the others are mere shadows compared to you."

"I'm flattered, but for some reason I don't believe you."

"What's it going to take for you to believe me?"

"Maybe if you kiss me, I can evaluate your truthfulness."

"Is there no other way?" I could feel myself giving in to that desire that I had been holding back.

"Do you really want another way?"

"No. Not really." I stepped close and pulled her against my body. Her eyes showed surprise as she felt my arousal.

"My. My. You are excited, aren't you?"

"Very much so." I leaned down and touched my lips to hers. Her tongue darted out requesting entrance. I complied, allowing her tongue to do a marvelous dance around mine. I felt her body push against mine harder. I released her and stepped back.

"What's wrong? I thought you were enjoying yourself?"

"I was, but if we don't stop now, I might not be able to stop later."

"Who says I want to stop?"

Her full and moist lips curved into a smile. There was a certain warmth in her eyes and when she spoke it was like a lover's caress.

Her hot breath fanned my fingers as she brushed her lips across my knuckles. I touched her cheek with my hand. She leaned her head into it. That lump returned to my throat.

"Why don't you kiss me? I know you want to?"

"I'm afraid of what a kiss might lead to."

"I won't let you do anything I don't want to do."

She reached and pulled my head down until I could feel her breath on my lips. Just a fraction more and they would touch. How long had I wanted to kiss her like this? How long had I waited for her to want to kiss me like this? Her lips parted and her tongue darted out to touch my lips. My mouth opened involuntarily. She continued pulling my head down until our lips touched in a glorious mingling of twirling tongues. I had never been kissed like this before. In fact, the only kisses I had in the past were chaste touching of the lips with Marjorie at the dance back in Rickety Springs.

I felt a tingling start in my lips all the way down and settle in my groin. I was sure she could feel my arousal. She pulled my body closer as she ground her pelvis into mine. I thought I would explode right then. She released me and backed away.

"You do want me, don't you?" she asked with her husky voice.

My voice broke as I answered. "I want you more than life itself."

"Let's go into the barn?"

I followed that beautiful form into the barn. She waited for me to get all the way in, then she pulled the door closed. She turned to me, reached behind herself and unfastened the tiny buttons. Her dress pooled at her feet.

CHAPTER EIGHT

Later I helped her fasten those tiny buttons. How the devil women worked those things is a mystery to me. I brushed the hay out of her hair, gave her a chaste kiss and watched her leave out the side door. I straightened myself up and went through the front door.

Buck Kendish, the foreman asked, "What'cha doing in the barn, Cavanaugh?"

"Just checking on some things," I told him. "I thought I might find them in there."

"You find what you was looking for?' as he looked to the side of the barn and saw Dakota walking away.

"Yep. I found just what I was looking for. Thanks for asking."

"Ain't you supposed to be checking the fence out on the east pasture?"

"Headed there right now. Thanks again."

"For what?"

"For reminding me that's where I'm supposed to be."

When I got back from checking the fence, I told Mr. Swenson I needed to go into town tomorrow.

"Sure, Brian," he said. "Anything in particular you need in town?"

"Got a little something I need to check into. I'll let you know if it works out for me."

The next morning, I left before anyone was up. I arrived in town just as the businesses were opening. I rode straight to the land office. It was locked up tight. What did I expect? Coming to town before anyone was open. There's one place that'll be open. The local saloon. I led Ranger over to the livery stable and left him.

I walked back to the saloon and went inside.

"You're here a little early, ain't you?" said Luther.

"I wasn't paying attention to what I was doing when I got out a bed this morning. How about a whisky while I wait for the town to wake up?"

Two men came dawdling through the doors. They sauntered up to the bar.

"Give us a bottle and be quick about it," the older one said.

"Be there in a minute," Luther told him.

"We ain't got a minute," he growled. "Now bring a bottle and bring it now."

"You boys need to bring it down a notch," I said calmly. "He said he'd bring it in a minute."

"That's okay," said Luther. "I don't want no trouble. I'm bringing it now."

"What're you butting in fer, stranger?" said the man. "We didn't invite you to this party."

"Maybe, I'm a party crasher," I turned toward him. "I was having a conversation with the bartender and you interrupted. That wasn't very nice of you."

"I'll show you nice. You're packing iron. Grab it."

Those were his final words. He fell backwards into his friend who quickly pushed him away.

"I ain't gonna draw, Mister," yelled the other man. "I ain't never seen nothing that fast. Who are you anyway?"

"Some folks call me Kid Cavanaugh. Maybe you've heard of me?"

"Sure have. I wish you had introduced yourself, when we came in here. Tebo might still be alive. If you don't mind, I'll mosey on outa here."

"What about your friend. You just gonna leave him lying there?"

"He don't mind. He's dead. He wasn't a real close friend. I figure the undertaker will come pick him up. So long," he turned and walked briskly through the doors. I heard him holler to his horse as he left town at a gallop.

"Ain't you kinda old to be called Kid Cavanaugh?" asked Luther.

"It sounds a lot better than Killer Cavanaugh, now don't it?"

"I reckon you got a point there. There's a rumor floating around that you're looking to settle down."

"Ain't no rumor. I'd be at the land office right now, but the only problem I have is folks won't leave me alone. There's always some smart aleck kid wants to kill me and make himself famous. I just want to be left alone. There wasn't no reason, no reason at all for this Tebo to die. Maybe I shouldn't have butted in."

"I figure Tebo was on the fast track to hell. Man like him, ain't long for this world. If it hadn't been you, it would have been somebody else on down the line. Anyway, thanks for standing up for me."

"What's all the shooting about?" the sheriff rushed through the door. "Who's the dead man and who shot him?"

"I reckon I'm guilty, Sheriff," I said. "Names Brian Cavanaugh. Man on the floor is Tebo, didn't catch his last name."

"Tebo Sterling. Got a flyer on him. Worth five hundred dollars. Looks like your lucky day," he said. "And then again, maybe not so lucky. After you collect the reward, I want you out of town by noon today."

"But Sheriff, it was self-defense. I saw the whole thing," explained Luther.

"I don't want a professional gunslinger in my town," said the sheriff. "Be gone by noon. Understand?"

"Understood," I shook my head. "Well, that shoots down my plans of buying a place and settling down here."

"Sure sorry 'bout this, Cavanaugh," said Luther. "If I could do anything I would, but he's the sheriff and he runs a real tight town."

"That's alright. I probably should be running along anyway. So long."

I walked to the livery stable.

"Bring my horse around, would you?"

"I figured it wus you. Recognized the horse. I don't figure you owe me nothing since you didn't leave him for the time you paid."

"You took good care of him, didn't you?"

"Jest like last time. One cup of grain and all the hay he wanted."

"Good. Now if you would?"

"Sure. Right away. If I kin ask, where you headed?'

"I really don't like to answer a lot of questions, but since you treated Ranger so nice. I plan on mounting up and go back to the Swenson Ranch for a little while, then whichever way he takes me."

"Must be nice to be so free. I sure would like to be able to do that. I'll git your horse."

He saddled Ranger for me. I mounted up and headed back to the ranch.

I rode into the barn and left the saddle on him.

I walked toward the house.

"Did you get your business taken care of in town?" asked Swenson.

"Well, Boss," I said. "It's this way. I ran into a little trouble in town and now I've got to be leaving the country."

"I'm sure it's something I can fix," he said. "You know I throw a pretty wide loop in this part of the country."

"I sure do appreciate that, but I don't think you can fix this," I told him. "I had to kill a man and the sheriff ordered me to leave."

"Yeah, that sheriff is sure set in his ways. If he tells a man to leave, you can bet he'd better leave," he said. "What about Dakota? You know how much you mean to her?"

"The way she feels about me and I feel about her is exactly the reason I've got to leave now, without seeing her. I can't be putting her, or for that matter, you in danger. That's what it would come to if I don't leave. Someone I care for deeply might get hurt. I couldn't live with that."

"I sure hate to see you go, but I reckon I understand. I sure dread telling Dakota that you won't be coming back. It's gonna break her heart."

"I'll get my things and be ready to leave in ten minutes," I told him.

I went in and packed what little belongings I owned and came back outside.

"Were you planning on leaving without even saying goodbye?" asked Dakota.

"Dakota. I don't know what to say. I care for you deeply, but I have to leave."

"I know. Pa explained it to me. I only wish it could be different. I've never known anyone like you. You touched my heart from the very first minute I laid eyes on you. I won't ever forget you. Goodbye," she turned and ran into the house, tears streaming down her face.

Talk about the weather imitating life. I heard the thunder clouds booming in the distance. The sun disappeared behind a black cloud and the wind started blowing up a lot of dust.

I looked at Mr. Swenson, nodded my head, mounted up and rode away from some of the happiest days of my life.

CHAPTER NINE

Being a fast gun ain't as much fun as I thought it would be. I enjoyed it in the beginning, but now?

That's the way my life went. In fact, the years went faster than one might expect. There were many occasions where I had to snuff out the life of a so-called fast gun. Each time it seemed I came closer to being a little slower. However, it doesn't always matter who's the fastest. It's who's left standing when the firing has stopped. And I always was the best shot around.

I could tell you stories for hours about the way my life was after I left the Swenson place, but there's nothing glorious about this kind of life. Sometimes I would go for months without having to face someone. Other times I would have to have a shootout as often as twice a day. I reckon if you averaged it out, I probably killed at least one man each day of my life. Not a very good thing to have written on your tombstone. There were a few times that stand out in my mind.

There was a time in Abilene. I was on my way out of town, having had an all-night losing streak at the Glory Hole Saloon. I was almost to the edge of town, thankful to be leaving this miserable place. I was just a little upset with myself for staying so long holding a losing hand. I had just ridden past the last building, when I heard the shot and felt it as it whizzed by my right ear. I fell from the saddle rolling and drawing my .45 as I hit the ground. I fired in the direction where I thought the slug had come from. My bullet found its mark as a young boy, couldn't have been more than 11 or 12 grabbed his gut, dropping a big Walker, Colt .45 as he fell face down in the dirt. I stood, turned the cylinder of my gun, pushing out the empty and replacing it. I slid it back into the holster and walked to the kid's body. A crowd of people were already gathered. It seemed folks always appeared after the fact.

"That's the Phillips boy," somebody said. "What's he doing carrying that gun?"

"Well, you know his pa was gunned down last year over in Palo Pinto County by a gunfighter," said another man.

The sheriff walked up to me shaking his head. "I told you when you came into town, I didn't want no trouble. I should a run you out then. Trouble always follows your kind. Now, I want you in the saddle and don't come back to my town, unless you want to face me. Understand?"

I nodded, watched as some men lifted the body and started carrying it down the street. I climbed aboard Star, pointed him away from the town and continued my journey. That kid was the youngest person I've ever killed. I still see him clutching his belly and falling down.

Another time I remember is the oldest person I killed. It was on a Wednesday night, around midnight. The reason it was so late was I had been having a winning streak at the Grifter's Saloon. I had just left the saloon when I heard my name called. I froze on the bottom step of the sidewalk, my hand moved immediately to my gun. I heard the voice call again.

"Yeah," I said. "I'm here. Whatcha want?"

"I'm gonna kill you, Gunfighter. Git ready to die," said the voice.

"You gonna face me or shoot me in the back?" I asked.

"You just stand there and sweat fer a spell, the way my boy did 'fore you killed him."

"Listen," I said. "If I killed your boy, it was a fair fight. I ain't never shot nobody without giving'em a chance. Now, why don't you come on out and let's talk about this. Nobody needs to die here tonight. How about it? You gonna come out? A man should at least get to see his killer's face, shouldn't he?"

I turned to my right as an old man, looked to be in his 60s stepped from the shadows. He was holding a double barrel shotgun. I felt the sweat as it began running down the side of my face and dripping off my chin. I was in a real pickle unless I could diffuse this situation quickly.

"Why don't you put the shotgun down," I said calmly. "And I'll buy you a drink?"

"Don't wanna drink with scum like you." he snarled.

There was just enough light shining on his face for me to see his eye twitch, which I knew from experience he was fixing to pull the trigger. I jumped to my left, drawing my revolver and fired, as the blast from both barrels almost tore the post from the building. The old man was jerked backwards from the force of the lead as if someone had a rope around him and pulled.

I stood, replaced the spent cartridge.

The only people to show up this time were the fellows I had been playing poker with and the sheriff.

"I saw and heard it all, Sheriff," said one of the players. "Old man Crenshaw had a shotgun and threatened to kill Cavanaugh here. He didn't succeed. It was clearly self-defense."

"Alright Cavanaugh, you survived another one. I just wish you'd done it in another town. I reckon you know what to do now. I want you gone by sunup. And Cavanaugh?"

"Yeah, I know," I said. "Don't come back. Right?"

"That's right," he turned away and walked over to the body. I saw him shaking his head as he looked at the dead man, then he turned and walked away, I suppose to get the undertaker.

I mounted Star and pointed him to the next town and hopefully a peaceful visit.

Now here I am, fifty years old and tired, very tired. I'm afraid if I don't stop now, I might not be able to stop the way I want to. I'll be stopped by a bullet.

So, I'm on my way back to the place where I had the most happiness. Just outside a little settlement called Rascal Flats to the Swenson Horse Ranch. I know after all these years, Dakota is married with half a dozen kids running around, but I only need to see her one more time.

As I rode through the gate that led to the main house, I made a detour to the big oak tree on top of the rise south of the house. I remember it was a beautiful place.

As I approached the tree, I saw two dirt mounds on the far side of the tree. I reined in Ranger and dismounted, dropped the reins and walked toward the graves.

I read the inscriptions written on the wooden crosses.

Baby Swenson. Dakota Swenson, age 21. Died in Childbirth.

She had lost her life, giving birth to our baby. She hadn't forgotten me.

I mounted up and rode down to the house. I walked up to the door and knocked. The door opened and an elderly man stood there.

"Brian? Is that you?"

"It's me, Mr. Swenson. I've come back. A little late, but I've come back."

"Come in. Come in. Marie. Bring some coffee into the parlor. I've got a surprise for you."

An old Mexican woman came in carrying a tray with two cups and a pot on it.

"Mr. Brian? Is that you?" asked Marie. "My goodness, what a surprise. You're looking just fine. I sure am glad to see you." She poured two cups of coffee and handed them to us.

"How you been, Mr. Swenson? Is the ranch doing alright?"

"I guess you rode by the big oak tree? She told me right before she died, that's where she wanted to be buried. She said that big oak tree was where she had some of the most enjoyable times of her life."

"I'm so sorry. I wish I could have been here for her."

"What are your plans now? Do you have any place special that you need to be?"

"I feel I don't have the right to ask this, but I'd kind of like to stay on here. That is if you'll have me."

"I'd like that, Brian. I been needing some help around her. I ain't able to get around like I used to. I figure if you've a mind to, you can run the place any way you see fit."

"I think I'd like that. Of course, as you know I don't have any experience in running a ranch, so I would expect you to guide me as I learn the ropes."

"Whatever you need, Son."

Well, it's been a little over five years since I returned. I haven't seen or heard anything about anybody looking for me. Of course, I have to stay vigilant each and every day.

I'm hoping that I can live the rest of my days, no matter how many that might be, in peace.

Epilogue:

Some folks might say this is a sad story. Yes. It is a sad story, however, when a man chooses to become a gunfighter, life isn't expected to deal the easy cards to him. If he had chosen a different life who's to say it would have been all roses. And even if his life had been rosy, we need to remember one thing.

Roses have thorns.

Other Books by J.C. Hulsey

Angel Falls, Texas

Velvet Sky, Arizona

Angry Orchard, Colorado

Clear Stone, Wyoming

Itching Tree, Idaho

Windy Butte, New Mexico

Devil's Dance, Dakota Territory

Redemption Road

Red Rose

Rebecca

The Concho Kid

Ugly Mugly

GUTSHOT

The Last Ride

The Old Man

The Pistol Preacher

Shortland

Dynamite

The Concho Kid

Dead Man's Gun

Does Nora Know

Doke Walker

Brothers

Satan's Refuge

Shadrack

The Brute

The Decision

The Greenhorn

The Gunfight

The Hangman

The Old Timer

Trudy

The Waterhole

Welcome to Texas Hell

Some Stuff I Wrote

Some More Stuff I Wrote

Even More Stuff I Wrote

Newest Stuff I Wrote

Brand New Stuff I Wrote

Brand Spanking New Stuff I Wrote

Look What I Found

Oldest Coon Hunter in Somervell Co
(Compiled by)

Confessions of a Battered Wife
(Compiled by)

www.ingramcontent.com/pod-product-compliance
Lightning Source LLC
Chambersburg PA
CBHW072119150726
47999CB00005B/2035